For the villagers of Hei Ni Gou
in Songming County, who inspired this story.
Page McBrier

To Sasha, my little sunshine.
Lyuba Bogan

Winter in Songming

by
Page McBrier

Illustrated by
Lyuba Bogan

Heifer®
INTERNATIONAL

www.heifer.org

It is winter in Songming. Fields once bursting with corn and potatoes lie still. The pepper bushes, their pods picked clean, stand patiently in low rows near a water cistern. In the soft valley, a lone rice paddy lingers, waiting for the churn of the plow.

Yet not all is quiet.

4

5

A rooster squawks outside the doorway of an old mud house. Inside, Zadou buries his head in his quilt and tries to ignore the racket. It's Saturday, and he's home from school for the weekend.

"Zadou! Get up. Don't you remember what happens today?"

Zadou peers out from the covers and sees his mother in the doorway, balancing a tub of water on one hip. "There's a lot to do before the workmen arrive."

6

Suddenly, he remembers. His feet hit the floor just
as Little Brother sticks his head inside the room.
"The concrete mixer is here!"

"It is? Why didn't anyone tell me?"

7

In the village, winter is a time when families make improvements to their homes. Zadou's family is adding two new brick and concrete rooms onto their existing house. The new living room and the bedroom for Zadou and his brother are already half-finished. Today, concrete will be poured for a second story.

Zadou throws on his boots and jacket and races outside. The mixer sits near a huge pile of gravel in front of the new kitchen. Standing on tiptoe, Zadou peers inside. Bits of dried concrete cling to the churning paddles.

"Don't touch," Little Brother shouts. "Father said not to touch."

9

"I'm only looking," Zadou says, but what he means
is he's only imagining. He pictures the machine filled
with gravel, and men adding water to the thick mixture
as the paddles churn around and around. He sees
workmen running back and forth to the ladder, handing
up buckets of fresh concrete. Then, pinching his eyes
shut, he imagines himself on the ladder, helping his
father re-examine the concrete corner to make sure
it's perfectly square and even.

In the village, everyone pitches in to build a house, but each man has his specialty. Setting a corner is a tricky job, one that requires detail and precision, and Zadou's father is the expert. Zadou knows this is a skill passed from father to son.

Zadou's daydream is broken by his mother's voice calling from the kitchen. "Son, where are you? I need you to peel some potatoes and chop some cabbage for breakfast."

He hurries inside and squats beside her on the floor, where she's already begun the potatoes. "So much to do," she mutters. Extra men are needed for today's work, and it is the family's responsibility to provide supper.

Zadou's mother begins to tick off the menu: potatoes with peppers, spicy chicken, pork and lotus root, sautéed cabbages and turnips, fish stew...

Hungry now, Zadou rushes to finish the potatoes and cabbage so he can eat. Outside, he fills the pot with water from the faucet, and then places the pot on the gas burner to cook. Minutes later, the vegetables are bubbling away.

15

While breakfast cooks, Zadou helps Little Brother feed the pigs. Little Brother fills the trough with ground corn as Zadou fetches fresh water. When they finish, they scatter more pine needles on the floor for soft bedding.

"They're here!" Little Brother shouts.

Outside, the men have arrived with a truckload of logs for the scaffolding. Suddenly, the courtyard bristles with activity. The family's neighbor Qin, who lives three houses away, is in charge. "Clear the courtyard," he orders. "Put the lumber over here."

With one eye on his father, Zadou busies himself moving a pile of bricks and staying out of the way of the workmen. It takes all morning for the men to balance the scaffolding and position the forms into which concrete will be poured. Once the forms are ready to be secured, Zadou's father climbs onto a ladder with his measuring tape.

18

Zadou watches from below. Will his father see him? Will he think the measuring is too complicated? His father extends the tape and presses it against the wall, mumbling.

Zadou stretches as tall as possible and then edges closer to the log ladder until he's practically touching the side. He waits, holding his breath, until...

"Ah! Zadou! It's you. Come here."

Quick as a cat, Zadou is beside him on the ladder. "You're old enough to learn this now," his father says, and Zadou nods. His father pulls the tape along the first edge. "Measure once, then twice, then a third time." Zadou pays close attention as his father teaches him how to square each distance to make sure the corners line up. If they are not careful, the walls will be crooked.

His father's friend Guo, who lives on the other side of the village, starts the engine on the mixer. It sputters, then roars, drowning out the men's cheers. Carefully, the men blend buckets of water into the gravel until it is smooth. Back on the ground, Zadou helps hand buckets of wet concrete to men waiting on the roof.

All afternoon, the buckets fly back and forth. Finally, when the concrete is poured and leveled, Zadou and his father climb the ladder one last time to check their measurements. Perfect.

Exhausted, the men clean up and help drag wooden tables and benches into the courtyard. The women arrive to help with the meal.

As dusk falls, the men crowd around the tables to eat. Zadou proudly sits beside his father. Women move in and out of the kitchen carrying steaming bowls of food. Children and mothers hover around campfires to stay warm.

At one of the tables, the workmen begin to sing, and soon another table joins in.

28

It's snowing in Songming. At first, there are only a few fat, fluffy flakes. They stick to Zadou's clothes like chicken feathers, and quickly blanket the courtyard. An old man says the snow foretells a good harvest, and the others nod, pleased.

Soon it will be spring. Zadou and his family will begin to prepare their fields with compost. They'll plant beans and vegetables and grass seed, and pick the last of the winter cabbage.

The snow falls harder now. Zadou's father pulls out an umbrella.
They laugh and huddle underneath. The sky is dark, lit only
by snowflakes falling into the fires.

It is winter in Songming.

Heifer International

1 World Avenue, Little Rock, AR, 72202, United States
www.heifer.org

As the seasons renew the Earth, so Heifer renews hope
in struggling families around the world. Since 1944, Heifer
has helped more than 9.2 million families in more than
125 countries move toward greater self-reliance through
gifts of livestock and training in environmentally sound
agriculture. The impact of each initial gift is multiplied as
recipients agree to "pass on the gift" by giving one or more
of their animal's offspring or the equivalent to another in
need. Visit Heifer.org to learn more about ways your family
can help end hunger and poverty.

Winter in Songming

Text copyright © 2008 by Page McBrier

Illustrations copyright © 2008 by Lyuba Bogan

Designed and produced by
  Verve Marketing & Design, Chadds Ford, PA 19317 USA

Printed on FSC Certified, 10% post-consumer paper,
using lead-free, soy ink: 20% soy or vegetable content.

Mixed Sources
Product group from well-managed
forests, controlled sources and
recycled wood or fiber
www.fsc.org Cert no. BV-COC-080720
© 1996 Forest Stewardship Council
FSC

Text is set in Goudy Old Style, Display type is OptiAmadeus
Printed in the U.S.A.

ISBN 978-0-9798439-4-5

Description of the work: Winter in Songming is a children's book for
3rd and 4th graders aged 9-10 years old. It tells of the approach of winter
in a small Chinese village, and the approach of a young boy's journey
toward adulthood. Award-winning author Page McBrier describes young
Zadou's excitement as he first watches and then participates in the
construction of an addition to his simple home. Lyuba Bogan's glowing
illustrations highlight Zadou working alongside his father and the other
men of the village as together they build something strong to see them
through many winters in rural China. Heifer International works around
the world in villages just like Zadou's to provide livestock and training
so that people may lift themselves out of poverty and into self-reliance.
With their newfound self-reliance, they are able to improve their lives
and the places they live, just like Zadou and his family.